Special thanks to
Emily Sharratt

Reading Consultant: Prue Goodwin, lecturer in literacy and children's books.

ORCHARD BOOKS

First published in 2020 by The Watts Publishing Group

3 5 7 9 10 8 6 4 2

A CIP catalogue record for this book is available from the British Library.

ISBN 978 1 40835 471 1

Printed and bound in China

The paper and board used in this book are made from wood from responsible sources.

Orchard Books
An imprint of Hachette Children's Group
Part of The Watts Publishing Group Limited
Carmelite House, 50 Victoria Embankment, London EC4Y 0DZ

An Hachette UK Company
www.hachette.co.uk
www.hachettechildrens.co.uk

BATTLE ON ALOLA

ORCHARD

MEET ASH AND PIKACHU!

ASH

A Pokémon dreamer who wants to have it all – including becoming a Pokémon Master!

PIKACHU

Ash's first partner Pokémon and long-time companion!

LOOK OUT FOR THESE POKÉMON

BEWEAR

GRUBBIN

TOUCANNON

ROWLET

BOUNSWEET

CONTENTS

PART ONE: CATCHING POKÉMON

PART TWO: STRANGE ALLIES

PART THREE: FIRST CATCH

PART ONE
Catching Pokémon

CHAPTER ONE

Grubbin

Ash wanted to capture his first Pokémon in the Alola region.

He and Pikachu were doing battle with a Grubbin, as Ash tried to catch it.

His new Alolan friends were cheering him on.

"Grubbin, the Larva
Pokémon," said Rotom Dex,
the new Pokédex that had been
given to Ash by Professor Kukui
at the Pokémon School.
"Grubbin is a Bug type,"
Rotom Dex continued.

Grubbin and Pikachu faced each other.

"It scrapes trees with its jaws and drinks their sap. It makes its home underground. Did you hear that, Ash?" said Rotom Dex.

"I sure did!" Ash replied excitedly.

Before Ash could tell Pikachu what move to use, Grubbin fired long strings in their direction.

"Pikachu, jump up!" Ash called quickly. His Pokémon just managed to leap out of

the way in time. "All right," Ash said next. "Pikachu, use Thunderbolt!"

Pikachu sprung into the air, then hit Grubbin with a powerful bolt of energy. The other Pokémon was shocked.

"In order to catch a wild Pokémon," Rotom Dex declared, "you have to throw a Poké Ball at it after it's been exhausted in battle."

Ash laughed. "That's right," he said. "Let's go!"

He took a Poké Ball from his bag and threw it at Grubbin. The Pokémon was hit and then pulled inside.

CHAPTER TWO

Pikachu Injured

The Poké Ball rocked once, twice, while Ash held his breath. Had he captured his first Pokémon in the Alola region?

Suddenly, Grubbin burst back out from the Poké Ball and burrowed straight underground.

Ash let out his breath in a disappointed huff.

"That's a shame," said Ash's friend Mallow.

"You were so close," agreed Lana, as they watched the earth being ploughed above where the Grubbin moved.

When they saw the movement stop, Ash pointed.

"Look, Pikachu! Grubbin is about to come back out. When it does, use Quick Attack."

"Pikachu!" said Pikachu in agreement.

They all watched, waiting in tense silence.

But when Grubbin burst back out, it wasn't where they were expecting it. After a moment, Pikachu sprang into action.

It bounded towards the other Pokémon.

As Pikachu ran, Grubbin shot more and more of the long strings at it. Pikachu had to dodge out of the way. One string caught Pikachu by the

leg, pulling it towards Grubbin.

"Watch out for its powerful jaws!" Rotom Dex called. As Pikachu was tugged along, it finally collided with the other Pokémon. Pikachu crashed to the ground.

"Are you OK?" Ash asked.

"Confirming damage!"
announced Rotom Dex.

CHAPTER THREE

In Bewear's Cave

Elsewhere on Melemele Island, a huge pink and grey Bewear stood outside its cave.

Inside the cave were Team Rocket: Jessie, James, Meowth and Wobbuffet.

They had been captured by the Bewear and now couldn't escape.

From time to time, Jessie would fling a Poké Ball at the Mimikyu that stood in the doorway of the cave.

But each time, the Mimikyu would bat the Poké Ball safely away.

"Look, Mimikyu," Jessie said in frustration, "you said you wanted to help us. Why won't you let me catch you?" She turned crossly to the others.

"Don't you even care? We need to capture that Mimikyu and get out of here before that Bewear decides what it wants to do with us!" As she shouted, James dropped a Poké Ball.

Jessie looked at it with interest.

"A Luxury Ball!" she said gleefully. "That's just what we need."

"Not that!" James protested. "It's part of my collection!"

"Too bad," said Jessie, cackling with laughter.

She span round and hurled the powerful Poké Ball at Mimikyu.

"A direct hit!" she exclaimed, as it struck the Pokémon and pulled it inside.

The Poké Ball rocked and then shone. Mimikyu had been caught! Jessie ran happily over to the Luxury Ball, which now had Mimikyu inside. As she reached to pick it up, a huge paw appeared in her way. She looked up to see Bewear towering over her.

PART TWO
Strange Allies

CHAPTER FOUR

Dinner Time

Before Jessie knew what was happening, Bewear had picked her up and tucked her under one of its powerful arms.

The massive Pokémon stomped back into the cave, with Jessie still held tight.

"Oh no," said Meowth. "Bewear says it's time for food."

"Jessie's not food!" James wailed.

"Mimikyu," Jessie cried in the direction of the Luxury Ball, "you have to rescue us. Please!" While her mouth was open, Bewear leaned forwards and dropped a smooth golden liquid inside.

At once Jessie's complaints stopped.

"What is that?" she asked in delight.

"I've never tasted anything so delicious!"

"It's yummy honey nectar," Meowth said, recognising it and opening its own mouth. One by one, Bewear fed them the wonderful honey, sending them into a happy trance.

Meanwhile, Ash, Mallow,
Pikachu and Rotom Dex were
at the Pokémon Center.

"I really need your help,
Nurse Joy," said Ash.

"Don't worry," she replied.

A Blissey Pokémon wheeled
Pikachu away on a stretcher.
"Pikachu will be all better in
no time," said Nurse Joy.

Rotom Dex was enjoying
refreshing its data with all
the new information at the

Pokémon Center.

"Rotom Dex, what's that Pokémon?" Ash asked, pointing to a small Pokémon that was flying through the air with a chain of flowers behind it.

"Let's see," said Rotom Dex, taking a picture. "That's Comfey, the Posy Picker Pokémon. It releases a relaxing scent from the flowers it picks. The scent has a healing effect and can cure many conditions."

CHAPTER FIVE

The Pokémon Center

Later, Ash and Mallow were having a drink in the canteen while they waited. Nurse Joy came in, wheeling Pikachu on a stretcher.

"I'm pleased to say that Pikachu is fully recovered!"

she declared. Pikachu leaped happily into Ash's arms.

"I'm glad you're all better, buddy," Ash said to his Pokémon.

"Let's check that," said Rotom Dex, seizing hold of Pikachu's tail. Startled, Pikachu released a bolt of electricity, giving them all a big shock. "Yes, Pikachu is back to normal," Rotom Dex croaked.

"Today's the day," Ash declared at breakfast time.

"I'm going to capture an Alolan Pokémon today for sure!"

"My data suggests that the best place to hunt for wild Pokémon today is the forest behind the school," Rotom Dex

told them.

"That could work," agreed Mallow. "The forest is where I first met Bounsweet." She smiled at her small Pokémon that was sitting on the table beside them.

"Bounsweet!" agreed the Pokémon, releasing a delicious smell into the air.

The scent drifted up into the air, capturing the attention of a passing flying Pokémon.

"Pikachu!" Pikachu cried in

alarm, as the flying Pokémon smelled Bounsweet. It hurtled down from the sky towards Bounsweet.

CHAPTER SIX

Bounsweet and Rowlet

Bounsweet spun its stalk around fast, stopping the new Pokémon.

"Who is that Pokémon?" asked Ash.

"Allow me," replied Rotom Dex. "Rowlet is the Grass Quill Pokémon. It stores energy during the day from the sun's light. It swoops down silently and unleashes a powerful kick."

As Rotom Dex spoke, Rowlet came in for another attack. It was beaten off by Bounsweet's spinning stalk.

"Hmm, it seems as though Bounsweet has noticed Rowlet, though," Rotom Dex observed.

The small Pokémon once again prevented the Rowlet's attack.

"That's because Bounsweet is used to it," said Mallow.

"Oh yes," said Rotom Dex. "Bounsweet is the Fruit Pokémon – a Grass type."

"It gives off a delicious scent. Lured by this smell, many flying Pokémon mistake it for a berry." Once more the Rowlet attacked and once more Bounsweet defeated it. This time Rowlet was flung backwards onto a power line,

where it swayed weakly.

"Maybe that Rowlet's hungry," said Ash.

As he spoke, the Rowlet wobbled again and then toppled off the line and towards the ground. With a gasp, Ash flung himself forwards.

PART THREE
First Catch

CHAPTER SEVEN
Food Thieves

Ash just caught the falling Pokémon in time. Carrying it carefully, he placed it next to a bowl of tasty fruits.

The Rowlet slowly opened its eyes and looked around. Spying the fruit, it leaped up and began to eat hungrily. Ash kept passing more and more food. At last the Pokémon stopped eating and gave a happy sigh.

Ash stroked the Pokémon gently on the head and Rowlet cooed, leaning into him.

Ash took a Poké Ball from his bag. "Hey, Rowlet – would you let me catch you?"

It looked at the Poké Ball, grabbed some fruit and flew off.

"Will you go after it?" asked Rotom Dex.

"You bet," replied Ash.
"Let's go!"

Back at Bewear's cave, Jessie
and James were looking around
cautiously.

"It seems safe," said James.
"This is our chance to escape!"

Just then, a chorus of shrill
noises made them look up.
A flock of flying Pokémon
hurtled past them and into the
cave. They seized berries from
Bewear's stash and then flew
off again.

"They took Bewear's food!" shouted Meowth.

"We have to get it back," said Jessie. Her friends looked at her in surprise. "Bewear fed us," she snapped. "Not helping would be against our evil code!"

"You're right!" the others declared.

CHAPTER EIGHT

Return of Team Rocket

Ash, Mallow, Pikachu and
Rotom Dex were getting tired
running after Rowlet. At last
they saw it land in a big nest
that was filled with three other
kinds of flying Pokémon. It
dropped the berries.

Rotom Dex leaped into action. "Pikipek," it said, hovering by the smallest of the Pokémon. "The Woodpecker Pokémon. It can unleash sixteen pecks per second to drill a hole into a tree."

"Trumbeak is the Bugle Beak Pokémon, and the evolved form of Pikipek," Rotom Dex continued, pointing to the bigger Pokémon.

"It attacks its opponents by firing seeds stored in its beak. And finally," Rotom Dex

perched by the biggest of the
Pokémon, "Toucannon, the
evolved form of Trumbeak.
Its beak heats up to over two
hundred degrees, and its peck
can cause a serious burn."

Just then, nets came flying from the trees, trapping the Pikipek, the Trumbeak and the Toucannon.

Ash looked in the direction the nets had come from.

"Team Rocket!" he said in disgust. "I should have known. Let Pikipek and the rest go!"

"I don't think so," said James. "They stole Bewear's food and we're here to take it back!"

Meowth fired another net, this time covering the stash of food.

"And we're going to take your Pikachu as a perfect present for our boss!" continued Jessie. "Mimikyu, attack!" she cried, flinging the Luxury Ball and releasing Mimikyu.

CHAPTER NINE

First Alolan Pokémon

Immediately, Mimikyu prepared to use Shadow Ball.

"Pikachu, Electro Ball!" Ash cried in response.

As Pikachu and Mimikyu battled, Ash muttered, "Rowlet, now's your chance to save your friends!"

Rowlet hurried to free the other Pokémon from the nets.

"Quick, attack again!" ordered Jessie.

Mimikyu obeyed, clobbering Pikachu until Ash's Pokémon fell to the ground.

"Mimikyu, finish this," yelled Jessie, and her Pokémon prepared to use Shadow Claw.

Suddenly, Rowlet spun into the air over Pikachu. The spinning created a swirling wind around both Pokémon.

The wind shielded them as it lifted Pikachu to safety.

"That move is Leafage," said Mallow, hugging Bounsweet.

"Are you OK, Pikachu?" asked Ash.

Pikachu nodded.

Just as Mimikyu got ready to launch another counter-attack, huge paws plucked Team Rocket and finally Mimikyu from the ground.

Jessie and James looked upwards.

"Bewear again!" they cried.

The giant Pokémon walked off, carrying Team Rocket with it.

"They're gone!" Ash said in relief.

The Pikipek were gathered around Rowlet, tweeting happily.

"Thanks for your help, Rowlet," Ash said.

"Aren't you going to capture Rowlet?" Rotom Dex asked.

"Rowlet has a lot of friends," said Ash. "I don't want to take it away from them."

As Ash and the others began to walk away, Ash felt an extra weight in his backpack. He looked round to see Rowlet nudging at a Poké Ball.

"Are you saying…?"

Rowlet nodded.

"OK," Ash replied.

He took out the Poké Ball. "Go, Poké Ball!" he cried, capturing the Pokémon.

"My first Alolan Pokémon!" said Ash, letting Rowlet back out and patting his downy head. "I'm so happy it's you!"

The End

DON'T MISS THESE OTHER OFFICIAL POKÉMON BOOKS